Dedicated to all the inventors, creators, and dreamers out there, but specifically Nicolas-Jacques Conté and Alexander Cumming. One created the pencil and one was granted the first patent for the flush toilet. This book would not be possible without either of you...
—BB

PENGUIN WORKSHOP
An imprint of Penguin Random House LLC
1745 Broadway, New York, New York 10019

First published in the United States of America by Penguin Workshop, an imprint of Penguin Random House LLC, 2025

Copyright © 2025 by Brett Bean

Penguin Random House values and supports copyright. Copyright fuels creativity, encourages diverse voices, promotes free speech, and creates a vibrant culture. Thank you for buying an authorized edition of this book and for complying with copyright laws by not reproducing, scanning, or distributing any part of it in any form without permission. You are supporting writers and allowing Penguin Random House to continue to publish books for every reader. Please note that no part of this book may be used or reproduced in any manner for the purpose of training artificial intelligence technologies or systems.

PENGUIN is a registered trademark and PENGUIN WORKSHOP is a trademark of Penguin Books Ltd, and the W colophon is a registered trademark of Penguin Random House LLC.

Visit us online at penguinrandomhouse.com.

Library of Congress Cataloging-in-Publication Data is available.

Manufactured in China

ISBN 9780593658970 (paperback)   10 9 8 7 6 5 4 3 2 1 TOPL
ISBN 9780593658963 (library binding)   10 9 8 7 6 5 4 3 2 1 TOPL

Design by Jay Emmanuel

Muk 'N' Honey

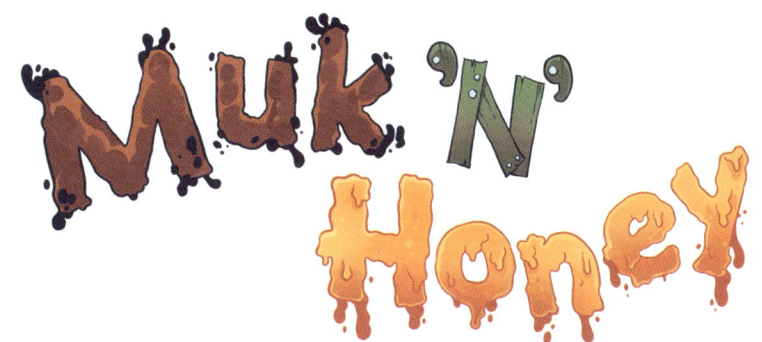

TREEHOUSE TROUBLE

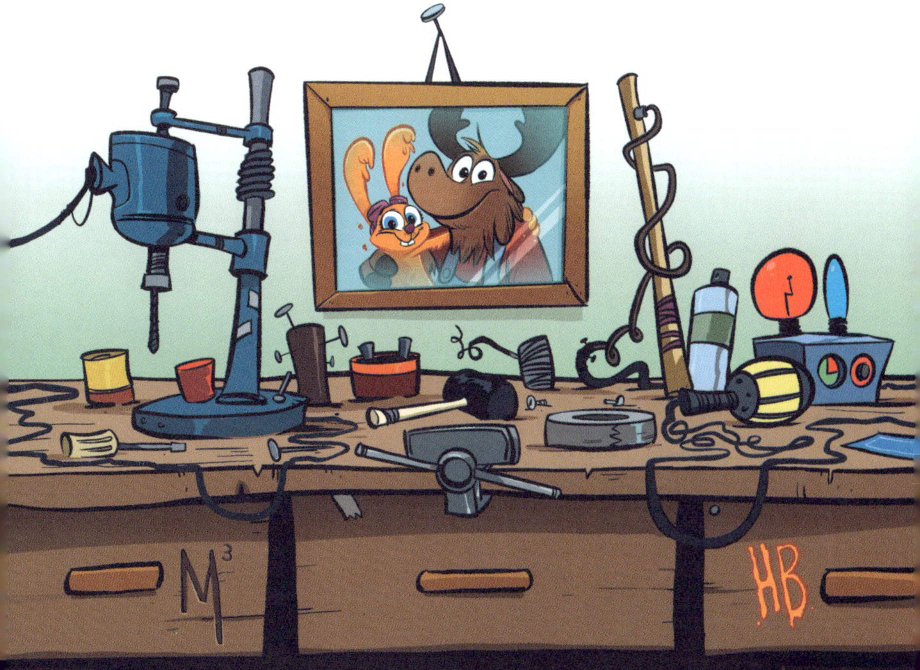

by **BRETT BEAN**

Penguin Workshop

Chapter 1

Triple-Decker Trouble

Here in the forest, there is a tree. But not just any tree. This tree is also a house. And not just any house, but a house filled to the brim with contraptions, doodads, and whatchamacallits.

But the most important thing in this tree that is also a house that is filled with inventions, is the most delicious and fantastical food creation the forest has ever known,

THE TRIPLE-DECKER HUNGER WRECKER

and it will be done cooking very, very soon.

And who created this TRIPLE-DECKER HUNGER WRECKER inside this house that's also a tree? That would be the forest inventors, Honey Bunny and Muk Muk Moose!

Honey Bunny and Muk Muk Moose love to tinker, experiment, and question, and they particularly love to use new inventions to help their friends. And right now, the entire forest is looking forward to their latest creation that's cooking away!

Which is a problem for Honey Bunny and Muk Muk Moose. Because as full as their treehouse is with gizmos and gadgets and the most mouthwatering food, it is also currently empty.

"Muk Muk, we have a problem," Honey Bunny said.

"Is that what's left of our treehouse's staircase?" Muk Muk Moose asked.

"Yes," Honey Bunny replied quickly, "but I was minding my business when it

collapsed. I had NOTHING to do with it!"

Muk Muk took a long, deep breath. Honey Bunny was the most brilliant partner a moose could ask for. But sometimes she got so excited about her latest ideas that she didn't take the time to think them all the way through.

"Did you finally try to test out the weight limit on our staircase?"

Honey Bunny looked up at him with her biggest bunny eyes and her best get-out-of-trouble smile.

The same smile she used the time she created the Room-Bat Drone to help tidy up but instead . . .

Or the time she created the Muddy Buddy Rejuven-8-Tor but instead . . .

Or the time two minutes ago when she absolutely, positively DID test out the weight limit on their staircase.

"Okay, okay, yes!" Honey Bunny confessed.

Honey Bunny hung her head. She hated feeling like she was letting her best friend down. Especially because none of HIS inventions ever seemed to explode.

But all Muk Muk Moose said was, "No one was hurt, and what's done is done. Plus, it seems like the stairs must not have been that sturdy in the first place."

"So, you're saying I actually did us a

favor by saving our friends in the future?" Honey Bunny perked up.

Muk Muk had already turned back to the problem at hand. "What matters now is getting back up to our treehouse before our newest creation is done cooking."

"AUGH, I almost forgot! Our first ever Triple-Decker Hunger Wrecker will be ruined!" cried Honey Bunny. "What are we going to do?!"

"We just need time to think it through." Muk Muk Moose stood tall. "We're forest inventors—we'll find a way."

Chapter 2

Tummy Grumbles

H**oney Bunny was** pacing. Not just her regular pacing, but pacing with the grumbliest of tummies.

"All of our work supplies are up in the treehouse! We can't build a new staircase from the scraps down here in time to save the—"

This is NOT good, thought Muk Muk, because nothing good ever came from a hungry bunny trying to think.

"All those layers!" sobbed Honey Bunny. "The eight cheeses, the colorful sprinkles, the experimental hot dog center . . . Muk Muk, we NEED to save the Triple-Decker Hunger Wrecker before it's too late!"

Muk Muk Moose closed his eyes and started to hum to himself. This was often his favorite way to put his mind to a problem. But Honey Bunny's best and most favorite spot to think was right in between Muk Muk's antlers! So Honey Bunny leaped onto Muk Muk's head and squeezed her eyes shut as tight as possible. She clenched her teeth and her fists, trying to make her brain work.

But Honey Bunny's grumbly tummy broke their concentration. "AUGH, my tummy needs solid food to process this much brainpower!" she shouted.

Muk Muk opened his eyes and scratched hard at his antler. Without any tools, he was unfortunately out of ideas, too. He was about to admit this when he saw old Mr. Figgy coming down the path to them.

"Forest inventors," Mr. Figgy exclaimed, "I've got a problem, and you are EXACTLY who I was looking for!"

Chapter 3

A Bowlful of Problems

"**Unless you've got** food on you, I don't want to hear about any other problems," Honey Bunny declared.

"That's just it," said Mr. Figgy, and he held out his bowl. "This IS about food! I have every ingredient in my bowl except the BEST one. I can't reach a single fig for breakfast anymore. My old legs just aren't what they used to be, and I'm hopping mad about it."

Honey Bunny bounded over to old Mr. Figgy in no time flat.

"And will you be sharing this breakfast of yours after we get the figs down?"

"Of course!" exclaimed Mr. Figgy. He proudly held out his bowlful of breakfast.

"You really need the figs to balance out the flavors," he croaked, smacking his lips. "But you're both welcome to a bite."

Honey Bunny looked long and hard at the mound of flies, wings, and oh-so-many legs.

Honey Bunny ruffled her ear. "I don't think I'll ever be THAT hungry!" she said and bounced as far away from the bowl of bugs as she could get!

"But if we're not sure how to fix our own problem yet, maybe the forest inventors can solve yours," she told him. "It's what we do."

"That's true," said Muk Muk as he thought up a most delightful idea. "Mr. Figgy, you say your legs aren't what they used to be. But what if we designed some way to jump even higher than any frog in the forest?"

"YES!" Honey Bunny squealed. "We can bounce our way to his morning munchies!"

Muk Muk started to scribble out his plan in his inventor's notebook. "I got the idea from seeing Honey Bunny hopping away from your terrible . . . uh, I mean scrumptious buggy breakfast, Mr. Figgy."

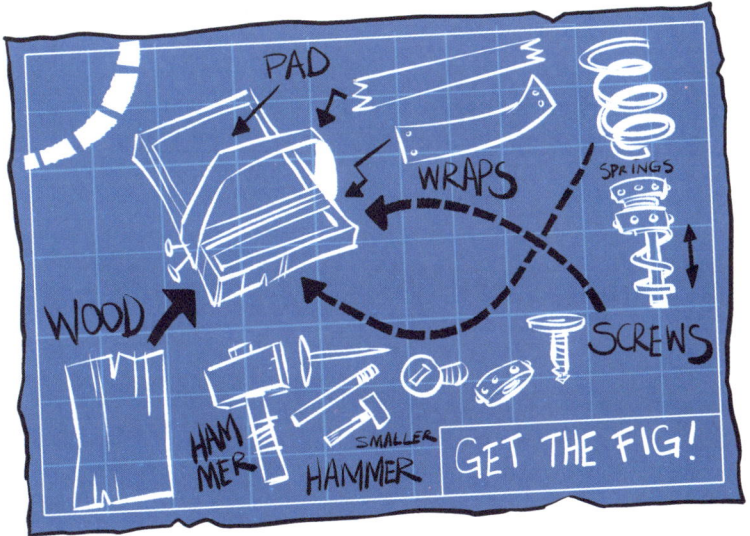

Honey Bunny gave a tail wiggle and a giggle. It was a brilliant plan. She loved how she and Muk Muk always knew just how to build upon each other's ideas. *It's not every day you find a best friend who can do that*, she thought.

Both inventors rummaged through the wreckage that used to be their staircase as old Mr. Figgy stared at his bowl, hoping for the perfect breakfast.

Honey Bunny twisted and pulled. Muk Muk yanked and cranked. And Mr. Figgy sat and waited. CLANG YANK

BOING
BONG
SCRAPE

The forest inventors had created the first ever . . .

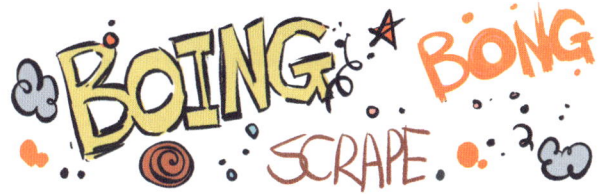

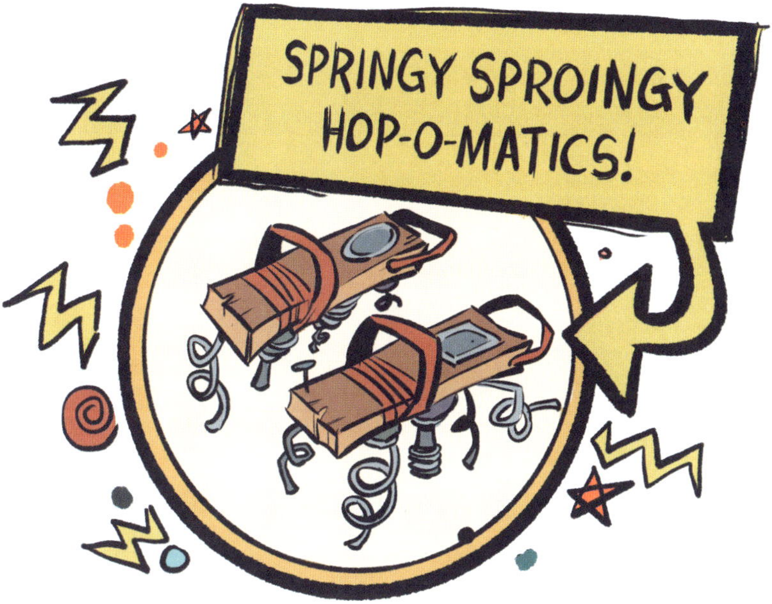
SPRINGY SPROINGY HOP-O-MATICS!

Muk Muk held them out with pride as Honey Bunny circled him in delight. He slowly strapped his hooves to their invention, and even though it took a little practice, he was bounding around the path in no time. One hop, two hops, and then with a third perfect spring, Muk Muk skyrocketed up into the fig tree!

And just like that . . .

. . . the invention had worked!

"Honey Bunny, I finally see why you love to bounce around so much!" He was quite pleased with himself as he plucked the perfect fig from the tree. Muk Muk dropped it down to the waiting frog.

Mr. Figgy caught it, cut it, and mixed it into his breakfast bowl. He took a big spoonful and jammed it into his mouth. "This is the best!" the old frog said as he gobbled up his yogurt, insect, and fig delight.

Muk Muk jumped down next to Honey Bunny with a spring in his step. She whispered to him, "That bug bowl is NOT a Triple-Decker Hunger Wrecker."

Their tummies grumbled as they watched Mr. Figgy eat, until he munched out the words, "Maybe them sprangy-sproingy-hoppity-do-shoes can help you with your treehouse problem?"

Chapter 4

Sproing into Action!

Honey Bunny let out a squeal and gave Mr. Figgy a gelatinous high five.

"That's a great idea!" she exclaimed. "Come on, Muk Muk! Bounce us up to the treehouse!" Honey Bunny jumped up on his shoulders and lowered her goggles.

Muk Muk Moose was less convinced this would work, although he had been wrong before. He wished he could take a moment to do

LET'S DO THIS THING!!

some calculations and make sure they would jump high enough, but he could feel Honey Bunny hopping ready to go.

"Welp," he said with a gulp, "if you commit to doing something, you should give it your all." So Muk Muk readied his goggles and shoved all his weight into the Springy Sproingy Hop-o-Matics.

"That did not go according to plan," said Muk Muk, his voice muffled by bark.

"Epic fail," Honey Bunny agreed as they both slid down the trunk into a pool of honey. Muk Muk stared at their newest invention. *These shoes have a use, but it's not to get up a treehouse*, he thought to himself.

Mr. Figgy had finished his breakfast bowl and hopped over to the lightly crumpled forest inventors. He sighed and patted his tummy. "Now THAT hit the spot. And I don't mean the place you smacked into the tree trunk."

He held out his bowl and spoon. "I'm sorry you didn't make it up to your treehouse, but here, you can take these in case they can be of use to you." Then old Mr. Figgy bowed, tipped his cap, and left.

Honey Bunny and Muk Muk Moose waved goodbye just as a delicious aroma wafted by. Honey Bunny could swear she saw the most delightful smells emanating out of the treehouse's windows.

"The Triple-Decker Hunger Wrecker is almost done cooking! We'd better think of something fast!" Muk Muk exclaimed.

Honey Bunny nodded. "Before it's too late!"

Chapter 5

The Prickly Patch Problem

H**oney Bunny started** frantically pawing through the mess of the broken staircase, hoping she'd find something, ANYTHING workable. Muk Muk Moose was pacing back and forth, trying to outthink their problem, when they heard . . .

Two small hedgehogs were running straight toward the forest inventors, the treehouse, and the Triple-Decker Hunger Wrecker that was still so far out of reach.

"Chalk 'n' Cheese! Slow down," Muk Muk said as Chalk, the older hedgehog, scurried up to him. Tears streamed down Chalk's face. "What's wrong?"

"We really did it this time, Muk Muk!" he squealed.

Cheese, his younger brother, leaped into Honey Bunny's arms with a splat. "We were playing around, and my Frisbee went over the briar patch!" he cried out. "And poor Chalk went in after it and came out looking like a reverse porcupine. Oh, I'll never forgive myself!"

"Wow." Muk Muk cringed, then said, "Take a deep breath, Cheese. Your brother is going to be okay."

Honey Bunny started to pluck out the prickles and spikes from Chalk, being extra careful not to hurt him. Muk Muk smiled. As fast as Honey Bunny liked to bounce around, she always focused when someone was hurting.

When there was only one spike left, she whispered, "Oh, Chalk, I am so sorry about this . . ."

"YEOWCH!" Chalk howled as he landed on top of his brother's shoulders. "I think I might need a new set of legs after all this!"

Chalk started to massage his sore rump and legs before pausing when he and Cheese suddenly noticed the staircase wreckage around them.

"Yikes! Honey Bunny, what did you do THIS

time?" they asked together.

Muk Muk giggled. Honey Bunny folded her arms and huffed, "Never mind what happened. But we can't be bothered by anything else right now! Now that you're feeling better, our REAL problem is getting

back up the treehouse, not finding your Frisbee, and I can't invent what I haven't thought up yet, and—"

I CAN'T THINK MY THOUGHTS!!!

"Don't worry," Muk Muk whispered to the young hedgehogs. "She gets like this sometimes but always does the right thing in the end."

Honey Bunny dusted herself off. "Yes, I am a bit overly dramatic," she stated. "All good bunnies are."

But as she watched the two little hedgehogs staring longingly toward their Frisbee stuck out in the briar patch, she twisted her ears, tossed her head back, and sighed. "Muk Muk is right. The forest inventors will help with your prickly patch problem!"

Chalk and Cheese let out a cheer as Honey Bunny and Muk Muk Moose brainstormed ideas together. But as the brothers waited, and waited, and WAITED, they began to get very bored. Soon the young hedgehogs started to wrestle and tussle, legs extended at all angles and one on top of the other. Honey Bunny turned to squint at them really long and really hard. "HOLD IT!" she cried out.

"THAT'S IT!" Honey Bunny exclaimed. "Chalk, you're going to get what you asked for!"

Chalk and Cheese were so confused that Cheese fell off his brother's shoulders. "What did she mean by *that*?" he asked.

But Honey Bunny was too busy to answer. She had already drawn up schematics and handed them to Muk Muk to review.

Muk Muk Moose nodded once. Then he bounded into the staircase remains and picked out the supplies they'd need.

They twisted and crammed, wrapped and shoved, pegged and pawed until they had made the forest's first ever . . .

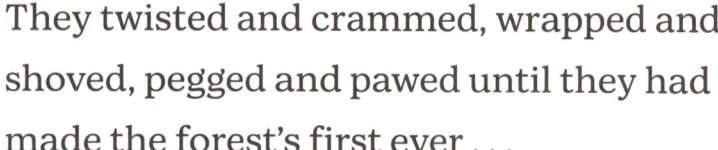

"You made new legs!?" Cheese exclaimed.

"You know it!" said Honey Bunny. "I got the idea from seeing you on

Chalk's shoulders. You were twice as tall! Why can't we do that, too?"

"As you can see, we can stilt our way over the briar patch to grab the Frisbee and none of the thorns will ever touch us," said Muk Muk as he wobbled to and fro on the Stilt-a-Tron 8000.

"You steer, and I'll grab!" Honey Bunny yelled as she scrambled up a stilt leg. Muk Muk trembled and looked down. They were quite high up.

"If this doesn't work, we'll all need new butts." Muk Muk gulped.

Honey Bunny jiggled in anticipation before she couldn't hold in her excitement any longer.

If it was up to Muk Muk, he'd go slow and steady, the moosey way. But if they were going to have a chance to save the Frisbee and the Triple-Decker Hunger Wrecker, they had no time for a safety

test. Muk Muk readied himself and gripped the giant stilts tight.

"Today we do this the bunny way!" he exclaimed before shutting his eyes and taking off.

The forest inventors put one long foot in front of the other as they crackled through the briar patch.

Chapter 6

What Goes Up, Must Come Down

Neither inventor felt a spike, pinch, or thorn. No one cried out or howled in agony. They both snuck a look down and realized their invention had worked.

"Not a doubt in my mind!" Muk Muk said. Honey Bunny just rolled her eyes.

They moved through the briar patch with ease, crunching and crackling as they went. It took them quite a few twists and turns to find the toy that Chalk and Cheese had lost. By the time they did, they had made a labyrinth of paths!

"Brilliant! Now ANYONE can come and go through the briar patch without getting a thorn in their side," Muk Muk said with a smile. Honey Bunny carefully slid down and grabbed the flying disc.

"Huzzah!" she cried out before climbing back up the Stilt-a-Tron 8000.

Muk Muk swung around and headed back toward the treehouse. Honey Bunny noticed he had become quite good at being this tall.

When they emerged from the thicket, Honey Bunny shouted to the hedgehogs, "GO long!" and tossed the Frisbee.

Chalk and Cheese were so happy to have their Frisbee back, they left their jump rope on the stump next to Mr. Figgy's bowl. "Take this in return for all your help!" Chalk said. And with that, they ran off, tossing their Frisbee back and forth till they were out of sight.

"A job well done," said a very satisfied Muk Muk Moose. He took a victory lap on the stilts and was feeling quite confident in them when he looked down at Honey Bunny. She was giving him a LOOK. The look she always gave him when she wanted to try something reckless.

"You want me to use the stilts to run straight up to the treehouse, don't you?" he asked. Honey Bunny nodded very fast. "And you're not going to drop this idea until we try it out?"

Honey Bunny shook her head so hard honey droplets went flying. She bounced up to his shoulders and wiggled her tiny tail in anticipation.

Groaning just a little, Muk Muk readied himself. "Well, we can try anything at least once."

So a very tall and wobbly Muk Muk,

with a very enthusiastic Honey Bunny on his antlers, bounded through the forest on the first ever Stilt-a-Tron 8000 toward the treehouse.

But instead of defying the laws of gravity, gravity let the forest inventors know that some laws can't be broken.

Honey Bunny's head popped out of the

rubble, and she shook her fist. "You win this time, gravity, but I'll be back!"

But before she could threaten physics any further, Honey Bunny heard a loud

coming from the treehouse.

Chapter 7

Bear with Us

The HISSSS and the POOF were letting everyone know that the Triple-Decker Hunger Wrecker was minutes away from being a giant disaster.

Muk Muk's head shot out of the wreckage next to Honey Bunny. "Between all the nasty smoke and a soon-to-be-exploding experiment gone wrong all over our walls, the treehouse will be a MESS!"

Now look who's being melodramatic, thought Honey Bunny. She patted him on the head. "We'll get into the treehouse. We just need to think BIG!" she exclaimed and popped out of the junk pile. "Now our brains are all warmed up from making those two new inventions. I'm sure we'll get the perfect idea any second now!"

MANY SECONDS LATER...

"No idea of what to do, or how to do it," Honey Bunny said. She slumped over the stump in gooey defeat. Muk Muk was already slumped in a lump on the other side of that stump.

"I'm too tired," said Muk Muk.

"And I'm too hungry," groaned Honey Bunny. "We might as well pack up, find another home, and forget the Triple-Decker Hunger Wrecker ever existed."

"Well, that's the wrong way to come up with the right solution," yawned a large and grumbly bear as he rustled out through the bushes.

"Bubbles!" Honey Bunny and Muk Muk cried out in unison.

Bubbles the Black Bear was about the nicest bear ever. He was also the slowest bear ever. He had just woken from his third nap of the day in the bushes.

"Awww boy, now THAT'S the spot," he sighed as he stretched and scratched. "This Itch-o-Stick you made for me really works wonders. You forest inventors know your stuff!"

But all Honey Bunny and Muk Muk Moose could do was hang their heads in shame. "It doesn't feel that way today," moaned Honey Bunny.

Bubbles replied with an even bigger grumbly yawn. He tugged his ear and stared at them. "Well, what's your problem?"

"That sounds like a lot," Bubbles said. He thought for a long moment. "Have you tried doing nothing?" he asked.

Muk Muk and Honey Bunny stared at him, completely perplexed. The forest inventors didn't know how to answer his question.

So Bubbles calmly placed his Itch-o-Stick on Mr. Figgy's bowl on the stump and stared up at the treehouse. He closed his eyes and took in a deep breath. Once, twice, three times, he slowly breathed in and out.

But being patient was not something Honey Bunny knew how to do. Her legs jiggled and wiggled until she just couldn't take it anymore!

"Are you mentally hibernating right now?!" she cried as she zoomed around Bubbles like a gooey land shark.

Bubbles carefully held out his paw and stopped Honey Bunny in her tracks.

"Stop for a moment and listen to the forest," he said in his slow, sweet voice. "Honey Bunny, remember when you built a new bridge after the river washed the old one away? Muk Muk, you made the most comfortable couch for fishing at Loon Lagoon last season. And you can't forget how you two both taught the forest how to make the fizziest root beer ever!"

"Yeah, yeah," scoffed Honey Bunny, "but why does that matter?! None of that helps us right NOW!"

"You CAN'T win every time. It's not natural. You two are a great team, but even great teams get stuck sometimes." The bear let out a giant yawn. "Take a break, slow down, and do a bit of nothing."

Honey Bunny and Muk Muk Moose glanced at each other and shrugged. They didn't have any better ideas. So they closed their eyes and slowed down their overeager minds.

They felt the wind gently blowing all around them.

Muk Muk could hear the birds chirping all the way from the lagoon. And Honey Bunny timed her deep breaths with the river water rushing under the bridge nearby.

Bubbles was right. Taking a break and slowing down was calming AND inspiring!

Honey Bunny and Muk Muk Moose both looked at each other and smiled. Things weren't fixed yet, but doing nothing had made them realize something they did have: each other.

"No matter how many times we get knocked down, you always seem to hop back up," Muk Muk said. "It's what makes you a great partner."

"And you're a great partner because you always keep me grounded," said Honey Bunny. "I think we're finally ready to invent our way up to that treehouse!"

"To the Thinking Spot!" they cried out.

Chapter 8

The Thinking Spot

H](#)**oney Bunny bounded** up onto Muk Muk Moose's antlers again.

They both knew they came up with their best big ideas in their Thinking Spot, and now they were finally calm and collected enough to work together the right way!

Muk Muk hummed and started to sway back and forth.

And as he moved to his rhythm, Honey Bunny slid back and forth from side to side matching his movements.

They slid and swayed, and thought and

pondered. Eventually, Bubbles broke the silence.

"Welp, it looks like this bear did his job for today," he announced with a big stretch. "Seems like a great time for a good sit." So Bubbles slumped his fluffy rump onto the stump. And when a bear sits, they REALLY sit.

"Would you look at that?" Muk Muk said. He considered all the wonderful things that had just happened in that instant.

"YES, look at that!" Honey Bunny bounced about in excitement. "That was even better than doing NOTHING, Bubbles! That was EVERYTHING!" she howled and gave that big, sweet, lovable bear a honey hug.

The forest inventors grinned and, without needing to say a word to each other, gathered the stilts, bowl, springs from the shoes, and jump rope.

They snagged, cradled, roped, and yanked.

They pushed and pulled, hammered and nailed, twisted and turned until everything was in place.

Honey Bunny was so confident in their idea that her once-grumbly tummy was now filled with butterflies. Muk Muk Moose took one final look at the design and was no longer tired. This invention was just that exciting.

With one last high five, Muk Muk got into position to untie the jump rope. He could hear the Hop-o-Matics ready to shoot off, and he knew it was go-time. Honey Bunny cackled and nestled into the bowl. She started the countdown as she gripped the sides tightly and wiggled her honey tail.

"Ready in three . . . two . . . one . . ."

Honey Bunny soared through the air in a glistening blur.

On the ground, time stood still.

Any miscalculations would result in one super squashed bunny. Muk Muk crossed his hooves that he had aimed his partner perfectly.

"BULL'S-EYE!" Bubbles yelled from the stump as Honey Bunny flew precisely through an open window into the treehouse of invention. Muk Muk did a little moosey dance.

From high above them, Muk Muk Moose heard whizzes and whirls coming from the treehouse. *She is supposed to prevent the impending explosion of the Triple-Decker Hunger Wrecker right now*, Muk Muk thought. *What is she BUILDING up there?*

Honey Bunny burst the window wide open. "Get up here quick, Muk Muk!" And then she began to smile. It was the same devious smile she gave him whenever she had something reckless she wanted to try.

Muk Muk was so focused on that devious smile of hers, he didn't notice the loud "KACHUNK." But he *did* feel something slam into his nose. And when he looked down, he had a plunger stuck to his face.

He landed in a heap on the kitchen floor. When he was eventually able to raise his dizzy head, Muk Muk saw the Triple-Decker Hunger Wrecker had cooked so large no one animal could ever lift it! Honey Bunny had already whipped out their creation station cooking utensils.

"Let's save the YUM!!" she cried. And together, the two forest inventors slowly removed the Triple-Decker Hunger Wrecker from the burner without a moment to spare. It was cooked to perfection.

Chapter 9
The Taste of Success

Later that day, the forest inventors sat with their friends at Loon Lagoon.

They invited the entire forest to try out their tasty new creation.

Each layer was filled to the brim with flavors and smells. If eaten in the correct order, from top to bottom, you'd get to enjoy a full seven-course meal with dessert at the end.

TRIPLE-DECKER HUNGER WRECKER
- TATER TOT FRENCH FRY MEDLEY
- HOT DOG
- CHEESE-BEAN TACO
- PB+J
- PIZZA
- SPAGHETTI MEATBALL
- MARBLED CUPCAKE FROSTING

Mr. Figgy sat on the most comfortable part of the couch, sipping a root beer and patting his tummy. "You two really know how to throw a party."

"All I know is we deserve a day off," Honey Bunny said, melting back into the couch. She took her last bite of cheese-and-bean taco.

Muk Muk agreed as he finished his dessert layer of marbled cupcake frosting.

Eventually, every animal had eaten their fill. The Triple-Decker Hunger Wrecker was truly a great invention.

But Chalk and Cheese, old Mr. Figgy, and even Bubbles were more impressed with the newest creation that sat over the lagoon.

Honey Bunny and Muk Muk Moose had named it the Loon Lagoon Launchpad and used all the leftover parts they had gotten from their friends.

"Just our little way of saying thank you," Muk Muk said.

"It took all of us as a team to make today a success," said Honey Bunny, oozing happily in her sunny seat. "Now it's time to relax."

Bubbles calmly sauntered up to the launchpad. "Before you do," he said with a big stretch. "I've got just one question for you two forest inventors."

Bubbles plugged his nose and launched into the lagoon.

"Well?!" asked a very wet and impatient Honey Bunny.

"Yes, yes, what is it you need?!" muttered a soaked Muk Muk Moose.

"You ever plan on rebuilding that staircase so I can come and visit your treehouse?" Bubbles asked.

WE NEVER FIXED THE STAIRS!